For Devin and Bridget—JM

For those who love cupcakes and fairy tales—may you always shine.—LW

union
square
kids

NEW YORK

UNION SQUARE KIDS and the distinctive Union Square Kids logo
are trademarks of Union Square & Co., LLC.

Union Square & Co., LLC, is a subsidiary of Sterling Publishing Co., Inc.

ISBN 978-1-4549-4352-5

Library of Congress Cataloging-in-Publication Data

Names: Marr, Joan, author. | Watkins, Lala, illustrator.
Title: Izmelda the fairest dragon of them all! / by Joan Marr ; illustrated
  by Lala Watkins.
Description: New York : Union Square Kids, [2023] | Audience: Ages 3 to 6.
  | Audience: Grades K-1. | Summary: Izmelda the dragon is excited to meet
  an actual princess, but Princess Penelope is uninterested in tea parties
  and glass slippers--can the two find a way to get along?
Identifiers: LCCN 2022010595 | ISBN 9781454943525 (hardcover)
Subjects: CYAC: Princesses--Fiction. | Dragons--Fiction. | Stereotypes
  (Social psychology)--Fiction. | Behavior--Fiction. | LCGFT: Picture
  books.
Classification: LCC PZ7.1.M37264 Iz 2023 | DDC [E]--dc23
LC record available at https://lccn.loc.gov/2022010595

For information about custom editions, special sales, and premium purchases,
please contact specialsales@unionsquareandco.com.

Printed in China

Lot #:
2 4 6 8 10 9 7 5 3 1

09/22

unionsquareandco.com

Cover and interior design by Julie Robine

IZMELDA

The Fairest Dragon of Them All!

Written by
JOAN MARR

Illustrated by
LALA WATKINS

union
square
kids

NEW YORK

Izmelda had never seen a real princess.

But she'd read about them in fairy tales.

And she *really* wanted to meet one.

So, she packed a bag with everything she thought a princess might need and flew off to the nearest kingdom.

Where . . .

she found . . .

Izmelda snorted in delight.

A real-life princess!
Let's be friends! What should
we do first? A tea party? A twirl
contest? Apple picking? But only for
green apples—I know princesses
are afraid of red ones . . .

The princess backed away.
"Are you going to eat me?"

"Goodness, no!" said Izmelda. "I brought cupcakes!"

"Cupcakes?" The princess dusted herself off.
"Listen, dragon—"

Izmelda squealed.

Izmelda skipped alongside Penelope.

Penelope stopped short.

Listen—
I'm not some fairy-tale
princess! I don't talk to mirrors and
I'm not afraid of apples. I don't have a fairy
godmother, I can't turn frogs into people, and I'm
tired of tea parties! I'm on my way to a how-to-be-a-jester
class where I can just have fun and no one cares that
I'm a princess. AND I JUST WANT TO GET
THERE BEFORE THE WITCHES
FIND ME!

Izmelda sniffled. She clutched her pearls. She blinked back a tear.

All of a sudden, a witch showed up.

And another one.

And then, some more.

Izmelda crouched behind Penelope.

Great. The
witches are here.

Are they going to eat
us? Poison our apples? Put
a curse on us?

No. They
just . . .

Penelope sighed. "I'll never get through this crowd.
I'm going to be late to my class!"

Penelope nodded.

Penelope paused. She looked at Izmelda.

Penelope smiled. "Would *you* take me to my jester class?"

Izmelda clutched her pearls.

"Is that a royal decree?!"

"Not a decree," said Penelope. "Just a friend . . . asking a friend."

Izmelda snorted in delight. "Even better!"

So Princess Penelope discovered a solution to her witch problem.

Izmelda discovered that princesses-on-a-break were just as fun as princesses-doing-princess-things . . .

And together,
they discovered . . .

. . . how to make time for cupcakes.

Pen | Iz ♡

Until . . .